NURSE HITOMI'S Monster Infirmary 6
D0881863
IT CAN
IN YOU
CAUSE
AND LEA
REDNESS--
LIKE IN THIS
PICTURE.
Pool Safety Manual
(Reference Images Infirmary Teacher Mannaka Hitomi)
SHWIFF
Pool Safe
(Reference Images Infirma
PEOPLE
ESPECIALLY
AT RISK
SHOULD
WEAR
GOGGLES.
BLOODSHOT!!
EYES GET REALLY RED
GYAAAAA!!

NURSE HITOMI'S Monster Infirmary
6
presented by
SHAKE-O

WHISPER
GROSS PHOTOS ASIDE...
WHISPER...
BIG OL' EYEBALL-SENSEI...
I'M SO GLAD WE HAVE HEALTH CLASS BY THE POOL THIS YEAR.
WHISPER
THANKS TO THAT, WE GET TO SEE HITOMI-SENSEI IN A BATHING SUIT! WE'RE NOT WORTHY!
WHISPER...
JIGGLE JIGGLE...
SHE'S JUST BIG ALL OVER.
I'M BURNING THIS IMAGE ONTO MY BRAIN.
WHAT A HEALING VISION...
A SIGHT FOR SORE EYES.
30 Chapter

SEVEN SEAS ENTERTAINMENT PRESENTS

NURSE HITOMI'S Monster Infirmary

story by and art by SHAKE-O

VOLUME 6

TRANSLATION
Amber Tamosaitis

ADAPTATION
Shannon Fay

LETTERING
Roland Amago

LAYOUT
Bambi Eloriaga-Amago

COVER DESIGN
Nicky Lim

PROOFREADER
Shanti Whitesides

ASSISTANT EDITOR
Jenn Grunigen

PRODUCTION ASSISTANT
CK Russell

PRODUCTION MANAGER
Lissa Pattillo

EDITOR-IN-CHIEF
Adam Arnold

PUBLISHER
Jason DeAngelis

ISBN: 978-1-626923-57-7

Printed in Canada

First Printing: July 2017

10 9 8 7 6 5 4 3 2 1

FOLLOW US ONLINE: ***www.gomanga.com***

READING DIRECTIONS

This book reads from ***right to left***, Japanese style. If this is your first time reading manga, you start reading from the top right panel on each page and take it from there. If you get lost, just follow the numbered diagram here. It may seem backwards at first, but you'll get the hang of it! Have fun!!

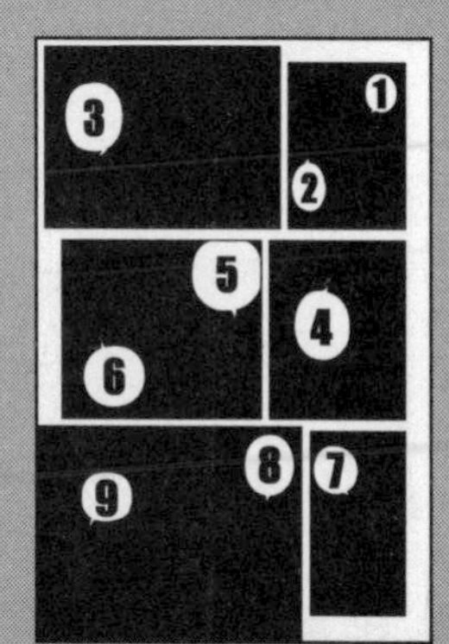

OMAKE MANGA "TOBITA-SAN'S FEVER"
AFTER CHAPTER 30...
HIS CHEST WAS SO HARD.
EVEN AS HE HELD ME, I COULDN'T FEEL THE FLUFF...
...
WELL, I GUESS YOU WON'T BE DOING *THAT* AGAIN!
IT WAS HARD...?
"THAT"?
YOU KNOW, HUGGING SENSEI...
SO STRONG...
HUG

TOBITA-SAN?
TOTALLY COOL.
LEAVE ME ALONE! I WASN'T IMAGINING ANYTHING WEIRD! DAMN, IT'S HOT TODAY, ISN'T IT?
FLAP! FLAP FLAP FLAP FLAP...
ばさ ささささ…
THE END

NURSE HITOMI'S
Monster Infirmary
6

SPECIAL★THANKS
MANAGING EDITOR IGAI-SAMA
FOR HANDLING PICTURES KURAYAMI-JOU-SAN KYUU ARIHITO-SAN YUMA MIZUKI-SAN
FOR 3D IMAGES USHI KANTO-SAN
FOR BOOK DESIGN, FROM AFTERGLOW NISHINO-SAN AND ETO-SAN
THE COMIC RYU EDITING DEPARTMENT, MARKETING DEPARTMENT, AND ALL OF THE BOOKSELLERS.
ALL OF MY READERS! THANKS FOR RECOMMENDING THIS SERIES TO YOUR FRIENDS, CONTACTING ME WITH YOUR THOUGHTS, AND TWEETING ME. YOUR FEEDBACK KEEPS ME GOING!
twitter:@shakekoujou
あとがき
AFTERWORD
GOOD EVENING, SHAKE-O HERE. THANK YOU VERY MUCH FOR READING VOLUME 6 OF NURSE HITOMI'S MONSTER INFIRMARY!
IT WILL BE FALL BY THE TIME THIS VOLUME GOES ON SALE IN JAPAN, BUT IT'S SUMMER RIGHT NOW AS I AM WORKING ON IT...HENCE ALL THE SWIMSUITS!
ALSO, SORRY FOR ALL THE PLOT PACKED IN AT THE END OF THIS VOLUME! THE STORIES OF HITOMI AND COMPANY'S MIDDLE SCHOOL LIVES WILL CONTINUE FOR A LITTLE WHILE LONGER.
IF YOU COULD LOOK FORWARD TO THE NEXT VOLUME, IT WOULD MAKE ME VERY HAPPY!
I REALLY NEED TO GET BACK TO WORK...
2016.10.13 SHAKE-O
KENSHIROU
SECOND YEAR OF MIDDLE SCHOOL
HITOMI
FIRST YEAR OF MIDDLE SCHOOL
(ONE YEAR BEFORE THE EVENTS DEPICTED IN CHAPTER 35.)

OMAKE
SINCE THE STUDENT COUNCIL BARELY GOT TO MAKE AN APPEARANCE IN THIS VOLUME, I DECIDED TO DRAW THEM IN THEIR SWIMSUITS!
LEVIATHAN

NURSE
HITOMI'S
Monster
Infirmary
6
To be continued......

"SENPAI"?
?
LONG TIME NO SEE!
DU-DUUUUN!
WAGH?!
SAKI...
SAKI-CHAN?!

...!

......
HEY...
SCRTCH

FLICK

I'M...
GONNA LOCK UP SOON, SO IF YOU DON'T NEED ANYTHING, SCRAM.
WAIT.
PAUSE
TATARA-SENPAI.

......
WHAT ARE YOU DOING HERE, HITOMI-SENSEI?
-AHHHH!-
NOTHING!
JUST GOT A LITTLE NOSTALGIC ALL OF A SUDDEN.

GAAAH! DID THE SCIENCE LAB ALWAYS SMELL THIS BAD?!
HEH HEH.
WE DID AN EXPERIMENT WITH HYDROGEN SULFIDE TODAY IN CLASS.
GAH!
GAAH!
LIKE-ROTTEN-EGGS...

I WANT TO GROW UP...

Middle School
Science Lab

HIC!
TET-SUGO...
NGH... WAAAAAH!
HEY, YOU'RE GETTING SOAKED, CRYING LIKE THAT...
DUMMY.
HIC!
HAVE A DRINK BEFORE YOU GET DEHY-DRATED.
UHH...
YOU...
REALLY ARE AN IDIOT.
SNIFF!
I'LL HUG YOU TIGHT UNTIL THE TEARS STOP.
TET-SUKO-CHAN...
HIC!
YEAH?
SNIFF...
I... I...

HITOMI ...?

Middle School

?

WE'RE NOT KIDS ANYMORE.
DON'T CALL ME KEN-CHAN.
LATER, HITOMI.
I'M GOING ON HOME.

I SEE, THAT'S RIGHT.
WELL THEN, THERE'S NO REASON TO TURN HER DOWN.
UH!
AH...
I'M HEADING HOME, TOO, KEN-CHAN, SO WAIT--
NOT TODAY.
AND...

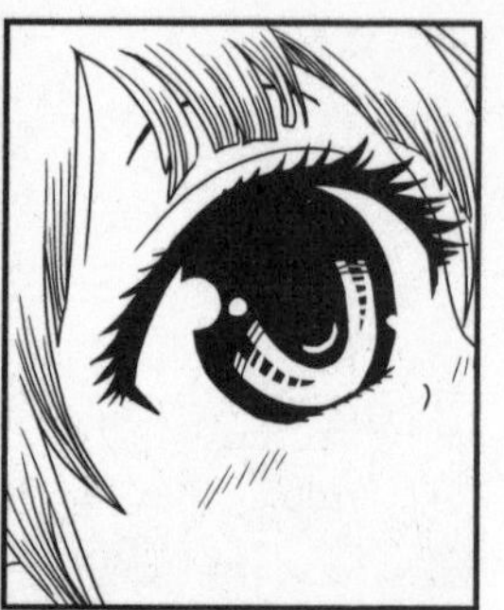
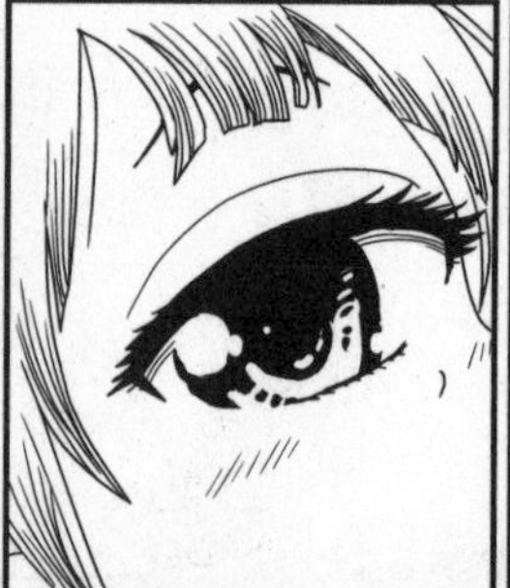
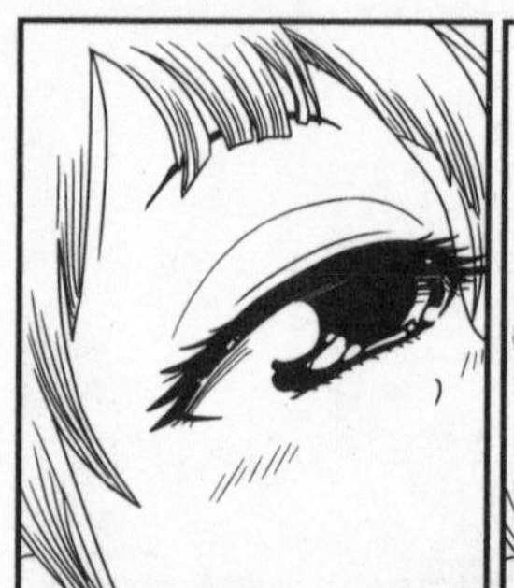

YEAH.

I'M...
JUST A CHILD, SO I GUESS I JUST DON'T *GET IT.*

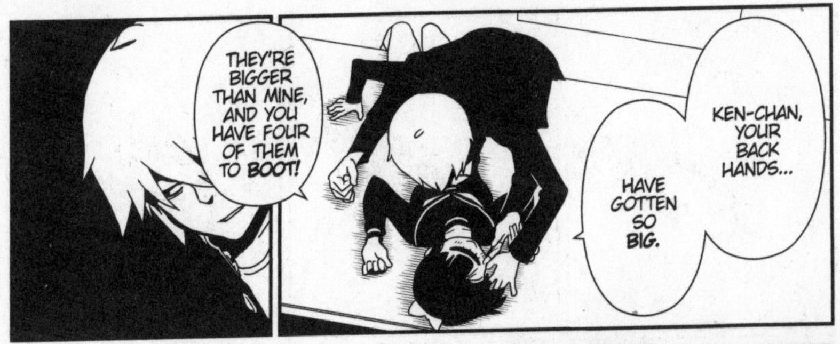
KEN-CHAN, YOUR BACK HANDS...
HAVE GOTTEN SO BIG.
THEY'RE BIGGER THAN MINE, AND YOU HAVE FOUR OF THEM TO **BOOT**!

YOU KNOW, KEN-CHAN, YOUR HANDS...
LISTEN, HITOMI.

ARE YOU *REALLY* OKAY WITH...
ME GOING OUT WITH YOUR FRIEND?

BLINK?
KEN-CHAN?
WHAT IS IT?

I KNOW, BUT...
I JUST WANT TO BE SURE.

HOW DO I APPEAR IN YOUR EYE?

...?

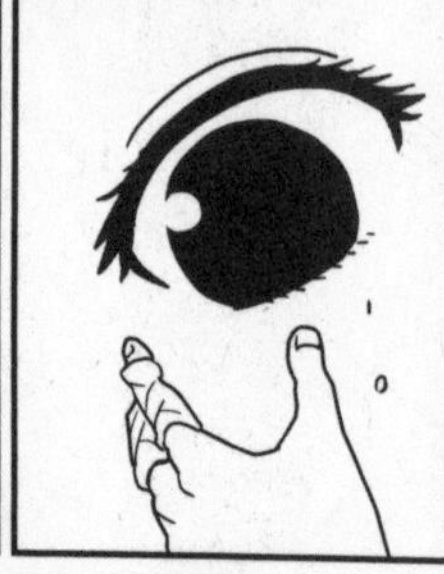

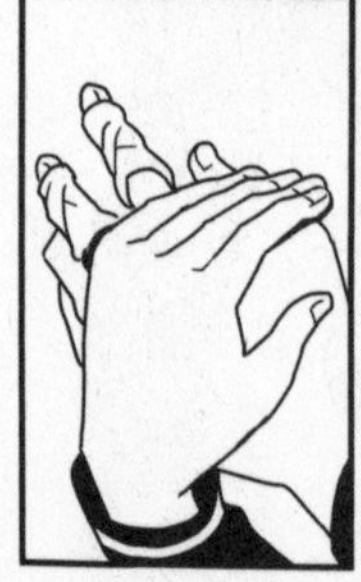

SAKI-CHAN IS SO SWEET...
KICK
KICK
YOU KNOW?
YEAH.

CLATTER
SHE HELPS ME WITH MY SCHOOL-WORK...
I KNOW.

EVEN WHEN I SAY SOMETHING STUPID, SAKI-CHAN NEVER MAKES FUN OF ME.
OOF!
SHE'S ALWAYS SO KIND TO ME--
I KNOW!
THWHAM

IT'S FROM SAKI-CHAN.
SHE'S BEEN A REALLY GOOD FRIEND TO ME...
SO MAKE SURE YOU READ IT!
......
......
YOU'RE GONNA READ IT NOW?
I GUESS I'LL BREAK THE RULES, TOO!
OOOF!

HITOMI, YOU'VE...
BROUGHT ME A LETTER FROM A GIRL I DIDN'T KNOW BEFORE.
I TOLD YOU I DON'T LIKE IT.

KEN-CHAN, WE'RE NOT SUPPOSED TO SIT UP THERE!
SHADDUP.
IF YOU'RE GONNA KEEP DOING STUFF LIKE THIS...
THEN...
......?
AH, NO! THIS ONE IS DIFFERENT!
...?

READ THIS LETTER...
OKAY?

AHHHHH!
I THINK I LIKE IT, TOO.

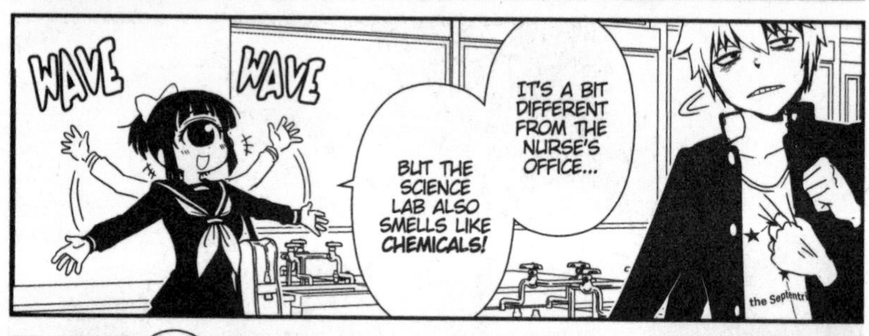
IT'S A BIT DIFFERENT FROM THE NURSE'S OFFICE...
BUT THE SCIENCE LAB ALSO SMELLS LIKE CHEMICALS!
WAVE
WAVE

......
TCH!
YOU'RE NOT WALKING HOME WITH YOUR FRIENDS TODAY, HITOMI?
CAN'T WE WALK HOME TOGETHER ONCE IN A WHILE, KEN-CHAN?
ALSO...
I WANTED TO GIVE THIS TO YOU BEFORE YOU WENT HOME.

AH!
HEY...
IS SAKI...?
?

SAKI-CHAN... SHE'S SHINING LIKE A JEWEL.

I KNEW YOU'D BE HERE.

I'M NOT LETTING A KLUTZ LIKE YOU ANYWHERE NEAR ME.
I'LL ASK KUROME-GAWA TO DO IT INSTEAD.
WAAAH!
YOU'RE PICKING ON ME AGAIN!
HUH?!
U-UH...
HA WA WA...
YOU REMEM-BERED MY NAME...?
BA-DUMP♥
BA-DUMP♥
...?
WELL, YOU DO HAVE A RARE LAST NAME.
UH, R-RIGHT...
SHE'S COOLING HIM OFF?
......

SLIIIDE
HUH?
THE NURSE ISN'T IN?
AH, KEN-CHAN!
WE'RE WATCHING THE OFFICE WHILE SHE'S OUT.
SPEAK OF THE DEVIL...
TATARA-SENPAI?!
BA-DUMP
ARE YOU HURT?
I HAVEN'T GOT THE HANG OF GRABBING THINGS WITH MY BACK HANDS YET.
IT'S JUST A JAMMED FINGER.
WHY DON'T WE FIX YOU UP, THEN?
......

......
GLANCE
HITOMI-CHAN, DO YOU...
HAVE SOMEONE YOU... LIKE?
HM?
SAKI-CHAN, YOU'RE SO NICE!
AND SO PRETTY AND GROWN-UP!
I LIKE YOU LOTS! ♥
BA-DUMP!!

I'M GLAD...
I LIKE YOU, TOO, HITOMI-CHAN!
AH HA...
HITOMI, YOU DUMMY, THAT'S NOT WHAT SHE MEANS BY...
GOOD GRIEF!
I GUESS YOU'RE STILL SUCH A KID, YOU CAN'T UNDER-STAND.
KNOCK KNOCK

YES, THAT DOES SEEM LIKE SOMETHING TATARA-SENPAI WOULD SAY.
YOUR BREASTS ARE BIG, BUT YOUR BRAIN'S STILL CHILD-SIZED.
WELL OF COURSE, HE IS THE CHILDHOOD FRIEND.
THEIR HOUSES ARE EVEN RIGHT NEXT TO EACH OTHER. IT'S LIKE SOMETHING OUT OF A MANGA!

I DON'T REALLY GET THIS WHOLE DATING THING EVERYONE'S TALKING ABOUT.
MEEEEH...
WHAT DOES IT MEAN?

UH...
WELL, YOU KNOW...
S-SAKI-SAN, CAN YOU PLEASE EXPLAIN IT SO EVEN THIS KID GETS IT?
WELL...
I GUESS YOU COULD SAY IT'S WHERE YOU AND THE ONE YOU LIKE DECIDE TO ONLY SEE EACH OTHER?

ARE YOU LONELY, TETSUKO ...?
SQUEEZE
I'M HERE FOR YOU!

MY~!
HITOMI... REALLY...
THIS IS THE ONLY PART OF YOU THAT'S MATURE!
MEEP! HA HA HA!
NO~! ST- STOP~!
WHAT A HANDFUL!
BOING
BOING
YOU HAVE THE BODY OF AN ADULT AND THE MIND OF A CHILD!
...
JEEZ!
NOW YOU'RE STARTING TO SOUND LIKE KEN-CHAN, TETSUKO-CHAN!
POUT!

OTONASHI-SAN SEEMS SO CALM AND MATURE, BUT THAT WAS PRETTY BOLD.
I DON'T GET THIS PART...!
EVERYONE'S PUTTING THEMSELVES OUT THERE...
I WANNA START DATING, TOO!
TETSUKO, DO YOU HAVE SOMEONE YOU LIKE?
I DON'T, BUT I'M ALWAYS LOOKING!
SAKI, YOU'RE SO LUCKY...

YOU'VE HAD *TONS* OF GUYS CONFESS TO YOU.
DON'T WORRY, TETSUKO. YOUR TIME IS COMING.

BUT WHEN?!

2ND YEAR OF MIDDLE SCHOOL
IN MY CASE...
I MOVED SLOWLY. MENTALLY SPEAKING, I WAS STILL VERY MUCH A CHILD.
YES... WHEN I WAS AROUND THEIR AGE...

I...
HAD MUCH TO LEARN.
TINGLE...
I HAD NO IDEA HOW TO HANDLE THE CHANGES I WAS GOING THROUGH...

SERI-OUSLY?
YES! APPAR-ENTLY SHE WENT AND CONFESSED TO AN UPPER-CLASS-MAN!

AFFECTION FOR ONE'S FRIENDS IS DIFFERENT THAN AFFECTION FOR ONE'S LOVER, ISN'T IT?
IS IT BASED ON WHETHER OR NOT ONE'S ATTRACTED TO THEM SEXUALLY?
SEXUAL FEELIN'?
UH, NOT EXACTLY...

HOW WE INTERACT...
WITH THE OPPOSITE SEX HAS ITS BASIS IN REPRODUCTIVE INSTINCT...
BUT I DON'T THINK THAT'S THE ONLY *DIFFERENCE* BETWEEN HOW WE FEEL TOWARDS FRIENDS AND LOVERS, YOU KNOW?
ESPE-CIALLY WHEN IT COMES TO LOVE DURING ADOLES-CENCE.

35
Chapter
ou are
dead ma

CLASS D, POOLSIDE

NURSE
HITOMI'S
Monster
Infirmary
6

YEAH, OKAY...

BUT LET ME SIT OUT NEXT TIME!
I DON'T WANT PEOPLE THINKING I'M A WEIRDO LIKE YOU GUYS.
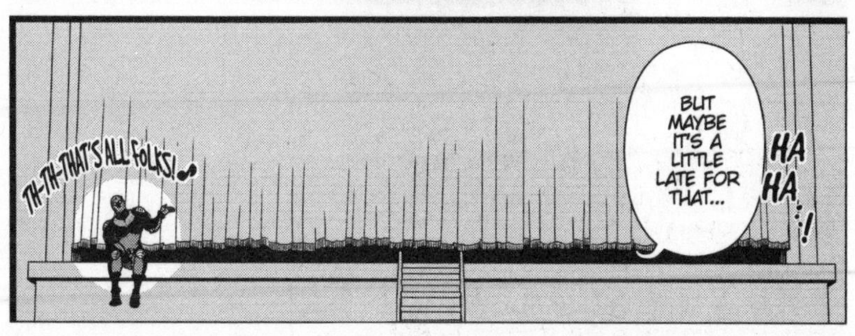
BUT MAYBE IT'S A LITTLE LATE FOR THAT...
HA HA...!
TH-TH-THAT'S ALL FOLKS!

SO LET'S ALWAYS...
TALK TO EACH OTHER!
'KAY, HIKAGE-SAN?

PEOPLE TELL STORIES...
BECAUSE THEY WANT TO SHARE THE REALITY WITHIN THEMSELVES WITH SOMEONE ELSE.
SO, JUST LIKE...

WHAT WE'RE DOING HERE!
RIGHT? ★

いっき
HEE
(re-) anima-
HEE!
いき♡
tion
SO, I'M SURE...
THAT THIS IS *OUR* REALITY! ★
......
THAT SEEMS LIKE AN AWFULLY SIMPLE TAKE ON IT.
WE ALL SEE THE WORLD IN DIFFERENT WAYS.
CONTINUING THE STORY FROM BEFORE...

I DON'T GET ALL THIS PHILOSOPHICAL MUMBO-JUMBO...
ABOUT CONFIRMING REALITY OR WHATEVER...
CLOP CLOP
HOP
BOING!
ちゃく
TUP
ALL I KNOW IS THAT I FEEL...
LIKE I'M LIVING MY LIFE WITH YOU, RIGHT NOW!

THEN THERE'S NOTHING I CAN DO.
FOR ME, THIS *IS* REALITY.

THAT'S NOT TRUE.

SO, NOT WANTING TO ACKNOWLEDGE SOMETHING AS FICTION...
IS WHAT ALLOWS PEOPLE TO BECOME IMMERSED IN THAT "OTHER REALITY"?
WHERE AM I RIGHT NOW...?

IF THERE'S NO WAY TO CONFIRM THAT THIS IS REALITY...
FOR EXAMPLE, EVEN IF THIS WORLD IS FICTION...

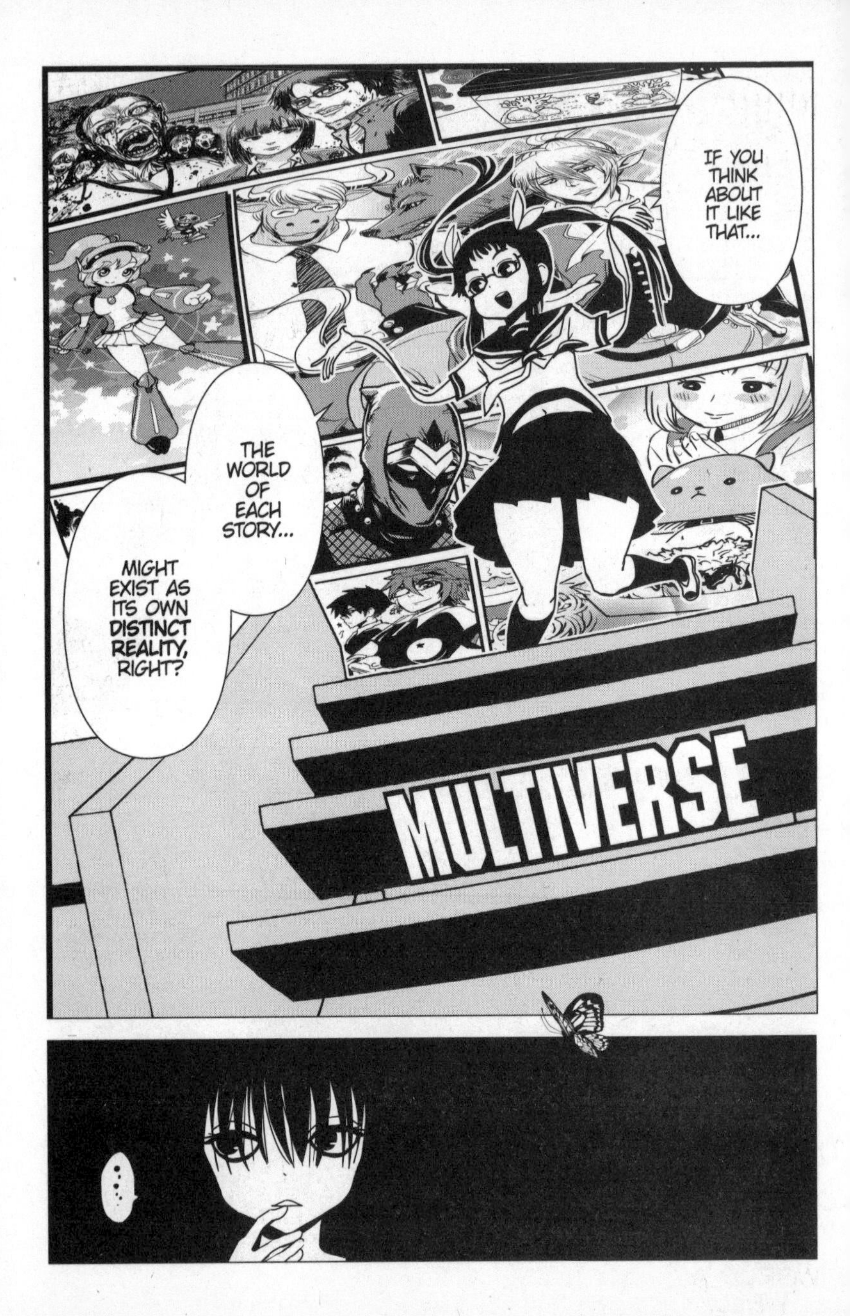
IF YOU THINK ABOUT IT LIKE THAT...
THE WORLD OF EACH STORY...
MIGHT EXIST AS ITS OWN DISTINCT REALITY, RIGHT?
MULTIVERSE
...

FOR A MANGA CHARACTER TO BE READING A MANGA THEMSELVES...
IT'S A LOT LIKE HOW WE'RE HERE, READING THAT MANGA...
TORA

AND IF THERE ARE READERS READING ABOUT *US*...
THOSE READERS...
THOUGH UNAWARE OF IT THEMSELVES, COULD BE CHARACTERS IN A FICTIONAL WORLD AS WELL.
MULTIVERSE
120

AND IF THERE ARE READERS READING ABOUT THAT WORLD...
THOSE READERS...
THOUGH UNAWARE OF IT THEMSELVES, COULD BE CHARACTERS IN A FICTIONAL WORLD AS WELL.

FICTION ACTUALLY *DOES* INFLUENCE REALITY...
AND THE OPPOSITE IS ALSO TRUE: A SERIES ONLY CONTINUES IF IT'S POPULAR IN THE REAL WORLD.
OR ELSE IT'S BROUGHT TO AN END, RIGHT?

JUST GO BACK TO YOUR OWN MANGA ALREADY.
OH, HEY...

ISN'T *YOUR* REALITY...
ALSO IN A MANGA?
THAT WAS JUST A HYPO-THESIS.

DOES THAT MEAN THERE COULD BE EVEN MORE LAYERS?
LIKE A *MATRYOSHKA DOLL!*
POP POP
POP PEEP

ANOTHER LAYER...?
HUNH!
YEAH, I SEE...

PEOPLE SEEK OUT STORIES AND TALES...
IN ORDER TO FUEL THEIR IMAGINATION.

Nurse Hitomi's Monster Infirmary
AND THAT WAS ANOTHER EPISODE OF *NURSE HITOMI.*
HEY?

THANKS TO THAT ANIME'S INFLUENCE...
HITOMI-SENSEI STILL BELIEVES SHE CAN SHOOT LASER BEAMS.
WHAT ?!

H-HEY, I DON'T...
REALLY BELIEVE THAT OR ANYTHING...
BUT...

WITH FICTION... THOUGH YOU KNOW IN YOUR *MIND* THAT IT ISN'T REAL...
IT STILL LEAVES A MARK UPON YOUR **HEART.**
IT MAKES YOU THINK THINGS LIKE...
"ISN'T THIS GREAT?" AND "WOULDN'T IT BE COOL IF I COULD DO THIS?"

I WANTED TO BE PURE CYCLONE.
PURE ★ CURE LOVELY ...!
PURE ★ CURE LOVELY!
ラッキーセブン
ピュア☆キュア
PURE CURE
CYCLONE...
CYCLONE...
KYUN KYUN KYUN...
KYAA!
BEAM!

OR AT LEAST, THAT'S SOMETHING I'VE THOUGHT...
AN ANIME...?
CALLED SOMETHING LIKE *NURSE HITOMI'S MONSTER INFIRMARY*?

HUH? NO, NO.
AN ANIME VERSION?
WELL...
WHEN YOU'RE A KID, THE LINE BETWEEN FICTION AND REALITY IS **BLURRY.**

AROUND THE TIME ONE HITS PUBERTY, WE HAVE A PRETTY GOOD IDEA OF WHAT IS REAL...
BUT EVERYONE MATURES AT THEIR OWN RATE, YOU KNOW?

I WANT TO BE IN AN ANIME, TOO!
DREAM BIG!

……
I SHOULD EXPECT NOTHING ELSE FROM THE CLASS D WEIRDO TRIO.
THOUGH, WHAT USUI-SAN IS SAYING ISN'T *THAT* RIDICULOUS...
GOOD THING I'VE GOT NOTHING IN MY BRAIN!
MY HEAD'S So LIGHT!
I DON'T THINK THAT'S A GOOD THING.
WE'RE NOT THE FIRST ONES TO WONDER...
IF THIS WORLD IS A STORY OR A DREAM.
What Is Reality?
IT'S A COMMON THEME IN MANY WORKS.
HONESTLY, IT'S A REALLY OLD IDEA.

REALITY AND FICTION CAN NEVER BE TRULY INDEPENDENT OF ONE ANOTHER, CAN THEY?
THERE'S ONE STORY I REMEMBER...

HEAD SPIN!!
WE'RE MANGA CHARAC-TERS?!
SERI-OUSLY?! ★
DON'T LOSE YOUR HEAD!
AHA HA HA HA!
あっはっはっはっは★

SO WHAT KIND OF MANGA IS THIS, THEN?
HORROR ?!
TWIST TWIST...
FUJIMI-CHAN, SOMETIMES YOUR CHEERFUL-NESS IS A BIT SCARY.

ACTUALLY IT'S MORE LIKE A SLICE OF LIFE.
THINK ABOUT IT...
WE'RE JUST NORMAL, KINDA CUTE MIDDLE SCHOOL GIRLS. NOTHING EXCITING EVER REALLY HAPPENS.
キメラ娘の日常
EVERYDAY LIFE WITH CHIMERA GIRLS

HMM...
NEIGH...

I CAN BECOME FLAT, RIGHT?
FLAP
FLAP
TO SAY IT FLAT OUT...
FROM A 2-D, PAPER-BASED PERSPECTIVE, THIS WORLD IS LIKE THAT OF A MANGA.
SO... WHAT IF "READERS" ARE WATCHING US...
FROM BEYOND THE FOURTH WALL RIGHT THIS VERY SECOND?
PEROPERO HORSE GIRL
PERHAPS THEY EVEN PEEKED INTO THE CHANGING ROOM?
HOW NEIGH-STY!
THOUGH, THEY AREN'T ALWAYS WATCHING.
......
WELL...
IF WE THINK OF IT AS AN ILLUSION, LIKE HIKAGE-SAN SAYS--
WHA~?!

FLAP FLAP
SO, WHY CAN YOU SEE THE FOURTH WALL, USUI-SAN?
WELL, MAJIRI-SAN...
I CAN TELL THE DIFFERENCE BETWEEN REALITY AND FICTION.
NO PROBLEM...
UNLIKE YOU, USUI-SAN.
A New Meeting
TORA
MONTHLY COMIC
3 BONUS TRADING CARDS
MONSTER MUSUMEN: EVERYDAY LIFE WITH MONSTER BOYS
Mad Shurikeen Trout Salmon

WELL, ABOUT WHETHER IT'S MADE UP OR NOT...

IT SAYS FROM THE START, "THIS IS A WORK OF FICTION," RIGHT?
HEY! HEEEEEY! WON'T YOU COME TALK TO ME?! I KNOW YOU'RE THERE!
......
★This is a work of fiction. Any similarities to actual persons,
ganizations, or events is purely coincidental.

THAT'S...
MOST MANGA HAVE THAT, RIGHT?
OF COURSE, WE KNOW THAT FROM THE START.
THEN IT'S RIDICULOUS TO HAVE TO START OFF WITH A WARNING TO PEOPLE THAT THE STORY ISN'T **REAL.**
THAT'S **NOT** WHAT IT'S FOR...
WHAT ...?

BREAKING THROUGH THE SUPPOSEDLY UNBREAKABLE WALL...
AND SPEAKING WITH THE AUDIENCE...
HELLO, ALL YOU READERS OUT THERE!
BECOMING AWARE THAT YOU ARE A CHARACTER IN THE STORY...
AND BEING MADE AWARE THAT YOUR WORLD IS A FABRICATED ONE...
SEE VOLUME 1 FOR FURTHER DETAILS.
WHAT COLOR IS YOUR BLOOD? THIS BOOK IS MONOCHROME, SO WE'LL NEVER KNOW.
IT'S GETTING PRETTY REAL, EVEN THOUGH THIS IS JUST A MANGA.
LET'S HURRY AND SETTLE THIS-- WE DON'T HAVE MANY PAGES LEFT.
IT CAN TAKE ALL THE FUN OUT OF THINGS.
IF YOU GOT ANY COMPLAINTS, TAKE IT UP WITH THE MAGAZINE EDITORS.

SO, MOVIES, TV DRAMAS, NOVELS, GAMES...
AND OF COURSE, MANGA...
HAVE A "FOURTH WALL" AS WELL!
YEAH, I'M GOING ON A DATE, BUT I DON'T HAVE A GET-UP LIKE THAT.
VIEWER
AESTHE-TICIAN
......
PLAYER
ZZZ...

SO, WITH THE WALL IN BETWEEN...
NEITHER SIDE CAN INTERACT WITH THE OTHER, RIGHT?
GAMES ARE DIFFERENT.

SO, IT'S THE BOUNDARY LINE BETWEEN "FICTION" AND "REALITY"?
RIGHT!
Fourth Wall
IT'S AN IMAGINARY, INVISIBLE LINE.

HMMM?
IN OTHER WORDS...
"YOU CANNOT SEE THE AUDIENCE FROM THE STAGE."
PANTO
MIME
CLOP CLOP
OR AT LEAST, THAT'S THE UNSPOKEN AGREEMENT.

WELL...
THAT'S THE GIST OF IT.

FLIP
Manga
Mad Shurikeen

LET'S ASSUME THAT THREE WALLS SURROUND THE STAGE...
DELINEATING THE RIGHT, THE LEFT, AND THE BACK BOUNDARIES.
1
2
3
4
Performance Don Quixote
BUT THERE'S NOTHING IN THAT FOURTH SPACE BETWEEN THE AUDIENCE AND THE ACTORS.
THAT'S CALLED "THE FOURTH WALL."

"THE FOURTH WALL"?
I THINK I REMEMBER HEARING ABOUT THAT IN DRAMA CLASS...
JUST LEAVE ME IN PEACE...
YOU MENTIONED THIS BEFORE--RIGHT, USUI-SAN?

MAJIRI-CHAN, FUJIMI-SAN, YOU REALLY WANNA KNOW?
I'LL EXPLAIN! WHAT IS THE FOURTH WALL?
IT HAS ITS ORIGINS IN PERFORMANCE TERMINOLOGY!

BON
BON
OKAY!
FOR EXPLANATION'S SAKE, CONSIDER A STAGE.
WEE!
B'A-BON

34 Chapter

Tale [teyl]

1. A falsehood or lie.
2. A story from long ago.
3. A work of prose literature.
   A description of events and feelings.

I HATE THIS KIND OF LAME META CRAP IN MANGA.
LIKE THE "STOP READING THE SYNOPSIS" BIT.
R-RIGHT...
2-D
MAY I OFFER MY THOUGHTS ON THE SUBJECT...
HIKAGE-SAN?
I ALREADY KNOW YOUR THOUGHTS ON THE SUBJECT...
USUI-SAN.
THIS IS THE ABSURD TALE...
YOU JUST WANT TO BREAK THE FOURTH WALL.
OF MY RIDICULOUSLY UNIQUE CLASSMATE...
AND ME.

#34 THE BUTTERFLY'S DREAM TECHNIQUE
LET ME SHOW YOU A BLISSFULLY PAINFUL DREAM
BETTER THAN ANYTHING REALITY HAS TO OFFER... ♥
Nonsense! Namu Amida Butsu!! Ninja Action!!!
SHURIKEƎN
マッド シュリケーン
Salmon is his favorite.
Salmon
rand New Volume 5
I...
THIS!

Last Time

In the subterranean city of Adachi, self-styled ninja Mad Shurikeen infiltrated the shady corporation Nishi Arai Matrix and had a showdown with corporate bodyguard Brain Vat!! Evading his virtual killing technique, Mad opted for his usual dirty tricks to completely annihilate the opponent...or so he thought!! In truth, it was all just a pheromone-based illusion from Papillon, a woman from the underground General Affairs division.

MAD SHURIKEEN

Mad-san is enjoying his solitary confinement by entertaining himself.

★This is a work of fiction. Any similarities to actual persons, organizations, or events is purely coincidental.

CLASS A, POOLSIDE

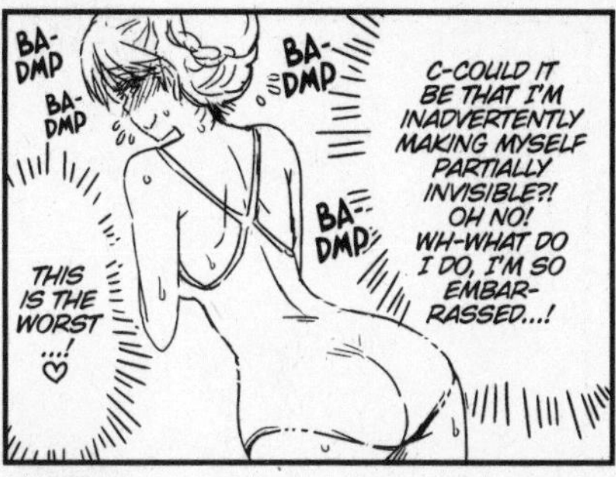

NURSE
HITOMI'S
Monster
Infirmary
6

DO YOU HONESTLY THINK I'D EVER SHOW THEM TO YOU?!
YOU'VE GOT THE ORDER ALL WRONG!!
WAAAH!
GYAA-AAA?! YOU'RE GONNA RIP 'EM OFF!!
EEEEEK!

WHAT DO YOU MEAN BY ORDER?
DO I NEED TO GET NAKED FIRST...?
WHA-WHA!
I... I DIDN'T SAY ANYTHING LIKE THAT!!
HEY!
WHAT'S GOING ON OVER HERE?

PERVERT!
THE WORST!
EVEN A GIRL IN HER BATHING SUIT WILL DO...
PEEKING IS ABSOLUTELY NOT ALLOWED!!
AT LEAST LET ME SEE HITOMI-SENSEI IN HER SWIMSUIT...
CURRENTLY IN REFLECTION
AT LEAST?! HOW ABOUT YOU AT LEAST SHOW US SOME SIGN THAT YOU'RE SORRY!
IT'S LIFE OR DEATH...

I WAS DAZZLED BY THE MOUNTAIN OF TREASURE AND I LOST SIGHT OF THE TRUTH...
THAT EVEN THE SMALLEST GEMS HAVE AN IRRE-PLACEABLE SPARKLE.
BA-DUMP

CLASS REP...
WON'T YOU LET ME SEE YOUR...
PRECIOUS JEWELS, YOUR PINK SAPPHIRES?

HANYUU-KUN...

YOU MIGHT NOT THINK IT'S A BIG DEAL, TO A PLAIN GIRL LIKE ME...
YOU MIGHT THINK, "WHAT DOES SHE CARE IF SOMEONE SEES HER?"
MY BODY MIGHT LOOK LIKE THIS FOR THE REST OF MY LIFE...
EVEN SO, I...
I...
I WANT BOYS TO... TREAT IT AS IF IT WERE SOMETHING PRECIOUS, AS WELL.
......
RUSTLE
YOU'RE PROBABLY RIGHT, CLASS REP.
TAKING A LOOK AT THEM WITHOUT THEIR CONSENT WOULD BE WRONG.

MM...
NO...!
NG...
THEY'RE SOFT?!
AH!
HUFF...
SQUEEZE
SQUEEZE
HEY!
L-LEMME GO...!
NO...

I CAN'T...
A GIRL'S BREASTS... HER NAKED BODY...

IT...IT'S SOMETHING THAT ONLY SOMEONE SPECIAL SHOULD SEE!
...!

NO MATTER HOW SERIOUS YOU ARE ABOUT THIS...
YOUR DESIRE IS ONE-SIDED.

AND THAT... THAT'S NOT LOVE!

NO!! I CAN'T LET YOU DO IT!!
AH!
BOI-YOING
BA-DUMP

PLEASE DON'T STOP ME, CLASS REP!!
I'M GOING...
ZWOOSH
FOR LOVE!
HANYUU-KUN...
HE'S TOTALLY SET ON THIS!
I CAN'T BELIEVE HE'S SERIOUS...
BA-DUM
BA-DUM
I... I HAVE TO STOP HIM, DON'T I?
BUT... WHAT IS THIS TINGLING IN MY CHEST?
I...
REACH

THEY ARE ALL PRECIOUS TO ME.
BOOB PARADISE
I WANT TO SCORCH THE IMAGES ONTO MY EYES... NO, ONTO MY HEART ITSELF!
......
ANYWAY, THE POINT IS THAT SLIPPING IN TO PEEP ON GIRLS IS...
WELL, NO ONE WOULD EVER EXPECT A BOY TO BE ABLE TO SLIP IN UNNOTICED, RIGHT?
WHA ...?
WH-WH-WHAT ARE YOU--?
I'M NOT HERE FOR ANY SHAMEFUL REASON.
TAP
?!
I'M HERE PURELY IN THE SPIRIT OF BREAST-ELLECTUAL CURIOSITY!
D-DON'T YOU MEAN "INTEL-LECTUAL CURIOS-ITY"?!
BA-DUMP

THANKS TO MY ABILITY TO INCREASE THE FEMALE HORMONES IN MY BODY...
BOOB LOVE
ESTROGEN
MASSAGE
SQUEEZE
MASSAGE
I CAN TEMPORARILY INCREASE THEIR SIZE!!
OPAAAA!
BOOBS ON DEMAND?!
THAT'S NO FAIR!!
NO, WAIT, LOOK, EVEN WITH THOSE HUGE BREASTS...
YOU'RE STILL A GUY, SO CHANGING IN THE GIRLS' LOCKER ROOM IS A NO GO!
HEAR ME OUT, CLASS REP!

NO MATTER HOW BIG THEY GET, THESE ARE STILL MALE BREASTS.
THESE BREASTS ALONE WON'T SATISFY ME.
THE ABILITY TO SEE THOSE FIRST BUDS OF MAIDEN-HOOD...
THAT ARE ONLY VISIBLE AT THIS POINT IN DEVELOPMENT IS WHAT FANS THE FLAMES IN MY HEART.

HUH? DID THE CLASS REP JUST DRAG SOMEONE OUTSIDE...?
H-H-HAN...
HANYUU-KUN?!
WHAT ARE YOU DOING IN THE GIRLS' CHANGING ROOM?!
SHOULDA KNOWN YOU'D FIND ME OUT, CLASS REP.
HEH!
AND, AND YOUR B-B-BREASTS...
AH HA HA HA!
I THOUGHT THEY DEFLATED! I MEAN, THIS MORNING THEY WERE TOTALLY FLAT.
HE WASN'T EVEN WEARING MAKE-UP THIS MORNING...
THESE ARE EXTENSIONS OF MY LOVE AND MY PHYSICAL CONDITION.

HEY, WHERE IS HANYUU, ANYWAY?
SLUMP
HE'S BEEN IN THE BATHROOM SINCE LAST PERIOD.
MAYBE HE'S GOT THE RUNS!

I CAN'T HIDE IT...

IT'S SO UNFAIR THAT THERE ARE SO MANY DIFFERENCES IN INDIVIDUAL SECONDARY SEX CHARACTERISTICS.
FIDGET FIDGET
STUPID GROWTH SPURTS...

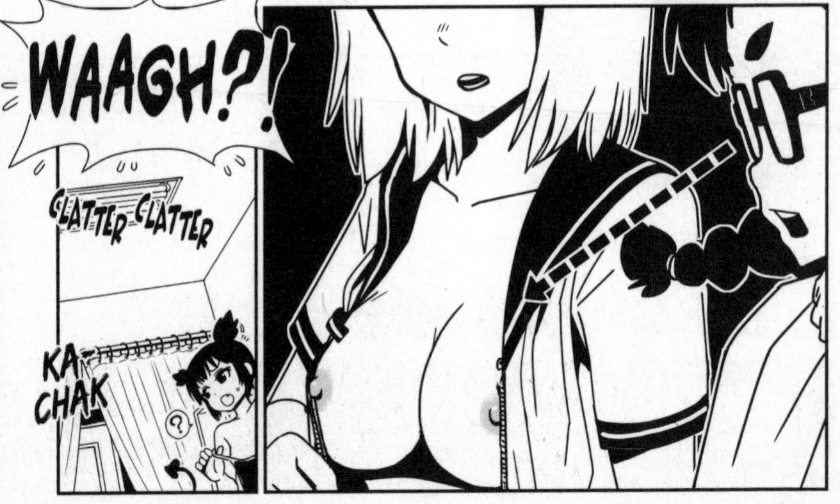
WAAGH?!
CLATTER CLATTER
KA CHAK
?

I HEARD HITOMI-SENSEI'S GOT HER SWIMSUIT ON!
SERIOUSLY?! LET'S HURRY UP AND GET OUT THERE!
DUDE, YOU'RE A TOTAL ANIMAL.
OOGI IN CLASS D IS *SUCH* A BABE.
AND OOKUBO IN CLASS B HAS A PRETTY SEXY BOD.
AND YET THE GUY WITH THE BEST FIGURE IN CLASS A...
SEEMS TO HAVE DEFLATED.

DID YOU SEE MOJI-SENSEI?
NO WAY! THAT *HAD* TO BE SOMEONE ELSE, RIGHT?!
YAO-CHAN'S UNDERWEAR IS SO MATURE...
HEY, HAVE YOU LOST WEIGHT?
HUH? YOU CAN TELL?
*UGH... I HATE WEARING REVEALING STUFF. SWIM CLASS IS THE **WORST!***

SAA...
I'VE BEEN WAITING ALL DAY FOR SWIM CLASS!
GLANCE
GLANCE
EXCITEMENT IS POUNDING THROUGH MY CHEST!
BA-DUMP
IT'S SWELLING, EVEN!!

33
Chapter
THE BOY WITH BREASTS
HANYUU-KUN
A GENTLEMAN WHO ENJOYS BOOBS. HIS BREASTS GREW SUDDENLY, BUT AFTER THAT, HIS HORMONES BALANCED OUT AND THEY SHRANK AGAIN.
MAY
JUNE
JULY

CLASS B, POOLSIDE

NURSE
HITOMI'S
Monster
Infirmary
6

GIVE FUMI'S BIG SISTER A CALL EVERY NOW AND THEN.
OKAY?
BA-BAP
UH...

—THE NEXT DAY—

HUH? I'M LISTENING, ONEE-CHAN.
AND?
North Dipper Seven Stars
SHE SURE TALKS A LOT.
I THOUGHT YOU MIGHT KNOW SOME-THING...
ABOUT SOMETHING THAT HAPPENED LAST NIGHT IN YOUR AREA...
I HEARD KEN-CHAN WAS SPOTTED WALKING ARM IN ARM WITH A WOMAN...
THOUGH, IT'S NOT LIKE I CARE OR ANYTHING.
PBFFFF!
FUMI?! WHAT'S WRONG, FUMI?!
COUGH!
SORRY, ONEECHAN, THAT WAS ME...
COUGH!
WAIT, I CAN'T TELL HER THAT...

Caféレストランカブト
Café Restaurant KABUTO
SORRY FOR THE TROUBLE, KEN-SAN.
THIS AIN'T THE FIRST TIME I HAD TO DEAL WITH HIM.
BUT WHEN I INITIALLY HEARD ABOUT YOUR NEW JOB...

I THOUGHT YOU'D FINALLY GIVEN IN TO A LONG-HELD CROSS-DRESSING FETISH.
HEH HEH...
N-NO! IT WAS JUST HOW THINGS ENDED UP...!
I GOT DRAGGED INTO YOUR FIGHT...
AND NOW I CAN'T WORK!

I NEVER WANTED YOU TO KNOW ABOUT MY JOB.
BLUSH
THOUGH, I GUESS IT'S BETTER THAN LETTING MY SISTERS KNOW ABOUT WHAT'S BEEN GOING ON.
YOU'VE GOTTA KEEP THIS WHOLE THING QUIET, OKAY?!
FINE, BUT IN EX-CHANGE...

I'M SO SORRY...
FOR PUTTING YOU THROUGH THAT...
I REALLY... AM...
UGH...
I HATE SEEING YOU GET ALL TEARY-EYED. STOP, IT'S OKAY!
WIPE THAT UP!
SURE, IT'S OKAY...
BUT ONLY IF HE'S WILLING TO ADMIT WHAT AN ASSHOLE HE'S BEEN.
AS LONG AS YOU'VE REFLECTED ON YOUR ACTIONS AND WON'T DO IT AGAIN, I'LL FORGIVE YOU.
NEXT TIME, JUST COME RIGHT AT ME.
WHETHER IT'S TO CHAT OR FIGHT, I'LL TAKE YOU ON.
UM, I DON'T REALLY WANNA GET HIT BY THOSE THINGS AGAIN...
R-RIGHT. GOTCHA, NO FIGHTING.

IT'S GREAT HAVING A PLACE THAT MAKES YOU HAPPY.
WHETHER YOU'RE MALE OR FEMALE IS IRRELEVANT...
I REALLY HOPE...
THAT YOU CAN FIND SUCH A PLACE, MASTER!
WHEN YOU SMILE.

......
STERN...
OKAY, THAT'S NOT HOW THINGS WORK, YA SEE?!
STARING AT SOME-ONE FROM AFAR IS NOT A GREAT WAY TO MAKE FRIENDS.
YOU THINK STAYING OUT OF SIGHT MAKES YOU LESS OF A CREEP?
SORRY...
I'M...

WHAT DO YOU MEAN BY COMPLEX-ES...?

BECAUSE OF THESE THINGS SPROUTING FROM MY HEAD...
PEOPLE MISTAKE ME FOR A GIRL!

IF YOU DON'T LIKE IT, THEN *WHY* DO YOU WORK IN A PLACE WHERE YOU DRESS LIKE A GIRL?
WELL, YOU SEE...
SOME THINGS HAPPENED, AND, UH...
All our employees have **TWIN TAILS**
♂
♂
♂
Guys as Girls
Maid Café & Bar
ツインテイル
Twintail

BUT, YOU KNOW...

WHETHER THEY'RE MALE OR FEMALE...
YOU START TO FEEL LIKE IT DOESN'T MATTER SO MUCH...
YOU KNOW?

Guys as Girls
Maid Café & Bar
ツインテイル
Twintail
3F
WHEN YOU'RE HANGING OUT WITH OTHER PEOPLE AND HAVING FUN...

PHEW...
AH WELL.
RUFFLE
RUFFLE
I WAS TRYING TO PROVOKE HIM, SO I'M AT FAULT HERE, TOO.

IT WAS PRETTY BALLSY TO TRY AND FIGHT, EVEN THOUGH YOU HAD NO CHANCE AGAINST ME.

PATA
PATA
THAT WAS PRETTY MANLY...
FUMI.

......
SLUMP...
MORE LIKE, "WHAT DID YOU DO TO *FUMI-KUN?*"
WHAT IF HE'S INJURED?
HUFF...
HUFF...

BUT THAT KNIFE...!
YOU THINK SOME PUNK WHO'S NEVER BEEN IN A FIGHT IN HIS LIFE COULD HURT *ME*?
AND THIS ISN'T EVEN REAL.

......
SORRY... I GOT CARRIED AWAY AGAIN...
UUU...
I'M TRYING TO BE BETTER, I SWEAR...!

TCH!
SWISH

BWAM
YOU BAS-TARD!
WHAT DID YOU...
SWISH
DO TO KEN-SAN?!

IF YOU WANT TO SETTLE THINGS LIKE THIS, *FINE.*
BUT BE A MAN AND DROP THE WEAPON.
SOMEONE'S BOUND TO GET HURT IF THAT THING'S IN THE HANDS OF AN AMATEUR.
THAT FACE-- I KNEW IT...!
EVEN IF IT *IS* A FAKE.
SHUT UP!!
......?!
RUMI-CHA--
NOT YET!

......
CALM DOWN, IT'S JUST CIGA-RETTES.
THE PROOF WAS JUST FOR ARGU-MENT'S SAKE.
JUST CALM DOWN AND I WON'T HAVE TO CALL THE POLICE...
HAH HAH HAH! HAH HAH HAH!
HAH HAH
I *TOLD* YOU TO CALM DOWN.
KA-SHINK

IT SEEMS OUR LITTLE FARCE WAS QUITE EFFECTIVE.
I FELT LIKE AN IDIOT, BUT IT WORKED.

PROOF OF WHAT?!
I HAVEN'T... I HAVEN'T DONE ANYTHING...
I WAS JUST WATCHING.
YOU MEAN STALKING. YOU'VE EVEN FOLLOWED RUMI HOME.
YOU CAN'T SAY YOU WERE "JUST WATCHING."
RUSTLE!

JOLT
......?!
DON'T...
DON'T MOVE!!
KA-CHI

?!
SO, YOU *HAVE* BEEN PLAYING PEEPING TOM.
RUMI *SAID* IT FELT LIKE BEING UNDER SURVEILLANCE, AND HERE YOU ARE!

......?!

WH-WHY ARE YOU HERE?!
I WANTED TO GET SOME PROOF BEFORE YOU COULD RUN AWAY.
SO WHILE YOU WERE GLARING INTO RUMI'S WINDOW, I SNUCK OUT THE BACK AND CAME UP HERE.
OWL'S EYE

RUMI-CHAN...
CHAN...
WHY...?
WHY... WHY WITH THAT GUY?

SOMEHOW, MASTER...
I GET THE FEELING YOU'RE NOT LIKE THE OTHERS.
I GUESS I CAN'T JUST LEAVE YOU ALONE!

WAS THAT JUST SOME KIND OF STANDARD LINE?
BITCH...
SORRY, BUT I CAUGHT EVERYTHING.

—THE DAY BEFORE—

......
HMPH! HMPH!
WELL...
AS HIS CHILDHOOD FRIEND... I JUST THOUGHT YOU MIGHT KNOW, YOU KNOW?
TUG
TUG
MY BROTHER IS CLOSER TO KEN-CHAN-- I MEAN, TATARA-SENSEI-- THAN I AM.
HE PROBABLY KNOWS SOME-THING.
SLUMP...
I SAY THAT...
BUT LATELY, THAT KID... HE WON'T EVEN TAKE MY CALLS.
DON'T YOU THINK THERE MIGHT BE SOME REASON YOU CAN'T GET AHOLD OF HIM?
STRETCH
UGH! THERE COULD BE, AND THAT'S WHAT SCARES ME!!

WHAT THE --?!

—THE NEXT DAY—

AND THEN THEY WALKED OFF TOGETHER!
OH, IS THAT SO?

DO YOU THINK SHE'S TATARA-SENSEI'S GIRLFRIEND?
WELL...
I DON'T CARE IF SHE IS OR NOT!
WHY DON'T YOU ASK HIM?!
Nurse's Office
Come to me with your health questions!

IT'S TATARA-SENSEI!
SHUFFLE SCURRY
THOUGHT IT WAS A GANGSTER FOR A SECOND...

WHA...?
HUUUUUH?

COULD IT BE...?
THAT WE JUST SAW SOMETHING WE SHOULDN'T HAVE...?
...
GRR RR RR RR RR-

GLARE
YOU MAKIN' ALL THIS FUSS OUT HERE ON THE STREET IS BOTHERING OTHER PEOPLE.
!
OH!
OH!
...?!
IF YOU GOT SOMETHING TO SAY, LET'S GO SOME-WHERE ELSE.
IS HE YAKUZA?!
NO! THAT'S OKAY!
SORRY! WE'LL BE GOING NOW!

TOTALLY DRUUUNK
UH OH!
WHAT'S WITH THAT ATTITUDE? YOU'RE THE ONE WHOSE HAIR GOT CAUGHT IN MY TEETH!
AHHH...
......
I... I'M SO SORRY...!

......
SHFF...
THOSE STUPID DRUNKS...

WE SHOULD DO SOME--
WAIT, LOOK.

HEY, BIG TEETH...

NYAN! NYAN!
BUT I AM GONNA KEEP MY PROMISE TO TAKE RESPONSIBILITY FOR YOUR INJURY!
UNTIL I GET BETTER?!
WHEN YOU COME BACK, WE'LL WORK TOGETHER!
SQUEEZE~

OF COURSE YOU WOULD KNOW ABOUT A PLACE LIKE THIS, ITSUKI-CHAN.
Maid Café
TWINTAIL
3F.
I HAVEN'T VISITED IN A WHILE.
WANNA DROP IN, KAMINAGA-SENSEI?
SURE!
AH, THESE "TWIN-TAILS"...!
HYAAAGH, WHAZZAT?

Monster Musumen:
MUSHROOM PUP
SIGH...
KA-CHAK
STRIP STRIP...
!
GOOD WORK TODAY, RU-MI-CHAN!
NYAAAA!
MIYA-SENPAI...
I HOPE YOU'RE GIVING IT YOUR ALL AS MY REPLACEMENT!
IT'S MY JOB, SO I'M DOING MY BEST.
BLUSH
BLUSH
FIDGET
WORKING IN CUSTOMER SERVICE CAN BE HARD SOMETIMES...

EMBAWASSING...
AND THE FACT THAT YOU HAVE TO WEAR THOSE UNIFORMS...
HEH HEH HEH!
MAKES IT ALL EVEN BETTER.

HMPH!
OH YEAH?
ARE YOU SAYING YOU'RE NOT ATTRACTED TO GIRLS WHO DRESS LIKE MAIDS BY CHOICE?
NOT AT ALL!
IT GOES WITHOUT SAYING THAT YOU ALL HAVE A NATURAL CUTENESS TO YOU, TOO!

WELL, MIYA-CHAN DID BRING HER HERE, AND SHE HAS A LOT OF TALENT.
AND THOSE HUGE TWINTAILS ARE MORE THAN WORTHY OF OUR CAFÉ'S NAME.
TWINTAIL
3F.
YOU CAN GO ON UP AHEAD, RUMI-CHAN.
OH, OKAY.

WHAT'S WRONG, RUMI-CHAN?
I JUST GOT A CHILL...
DON'T WORRY... I'M FINE...
RUMI-CHAN, YOU'RE SO CLUMSY!
KEH HEH HEH!
BUT IT'S CUTE.

STARE.....
LIGHT STAFF
MANSION DE BROCCOLI

SHUDDER

I REALLY DO UNDERSTAND HOW PAINFUL IT CAN BE...
COMPARING YOURSELF TO THOSE AROUND YOU.

BUT THAT'S HOW I MET RUMI-CHAN.
AS WELL AS WHAT IT'S LIKE LIVING WITH A COMPLEX...

I'M NOT WORTHLESS...?

BUT THIS IS ALL I CAN DO.

PLEASE DON'T SAY...

THAT YOU'RE WORTHLESS.

OF COURSE I WOULDN'T END UP CHATTING WITH ANY **NORMAL** GIRLS...

NOT IN A SHOP LIKE **THIS.**

Chapter 32

......
HEADING TO WORK AT THE SAME TIME, AS USUAL...
HA HA
HA HA
I'M ALWAYS WATCHING YOU...
HA HA HA HA HA!
RUMI-CHAN!
LITTLE DEMONS

REPLAYING MESSAGE.
HELLO, FUMIO? THIS IS YOUR BIG SISTER.
ARE YOU EATING PROPERLY? IS COLLEGE KEEPING YOU BUSY?
YOU'RE NOT THAT FAR AWAY. COULDN'T YOU STOP BY ONCE IN A WHILE?
YOU KNOW, MITSUMI IS--
CLICK
VOICEMAIL
TCH!

BABY SISTER CAN GO ABROAD OR WHATEVER FOR ALL I CARE.
IT'S GOT NOTHING TO DO WITH ME.
Tigers Mansion Hatotama No.10
I GOT NO TIME TO WORRY ABOUT THEM.

Student Health Record
May 201X
Class 2-B
Okubo Anna
Void Face Girl
• There is a big
hole in her face
• Where that hole
Or what there might
nobody
knows
how it
• Her sense of smell
around the time that
breathing, voice,
functions are
intact
and her
• Below her neck
but
functional body, comparable to an adult woman's.
THE HOLE DOES
NOT CLOSE WHEN SHE
SLEEPS OR SWIMS,
BUT IT NARROWS WHEN SHE
DRINKS FROM A STRAW.

NURSE
HITOMI'S
Monster
Infirmary
6

KNOWING WHAT LIES BEYOND THAT DEEP VOID...
SWISH
TREMBLE
TREMBLE
IT'S LIKE UNCOVERING A SACRED MYSTERY.

MAY I...?
CALL YOU BY YOUR FIRST NAME... HASUMI?
ふあわ FUAWA

NYUU!
'COURSE!
IT'S NOT A BAD THING, FEELING LIKE YOU CAN FINALLY SEE...
SOME-ONE'S HIDDEN SMILE.

HUFF...
HUFF...
HUFF...
HUFF...
HUFF...
ZPFF
HEE HEE!

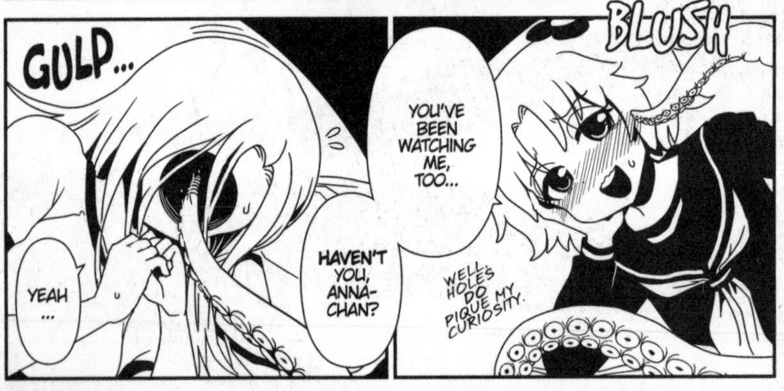
BLUSH
YOU'VE BEEN WATCHING ME, TOO...
HAVEN'T YOU, ANNA-CHAN?
WELL, HOLES DO PIQUE MY CURIOSITY.
GULP...
YEAH ...

YOU'RE A LOT BOLDER THAN I EXPECTED!
SORRY IF I CAME ON TOO STRONG...
I...I DON'T HAVE A FACE TO SHOW MY EXPRESSIONS, SO IF I CAN'T PUT WHAT I WANT INTO WORDS...
I ALSO... UHM...
OKUTOU-SAN...

NYAAAA!
SOOOO MYSTERIOUS?!
I THINK OKUBO-SAN'S SO INTERESTING! ♪
RUB
RUB
BA-DUMP
AHA HA! YOU'RE SO WEIRD, HATCHAN.
HUH? AREN'T YOU CURIOUS?
BA-DUMP
BA-DUMP
BA-DUMP
GLANCE
GLANCE
BA-DUMP
OKUBO-SAN?!
DAAAZE

WHEN I WAS IN ELEMENTARY SCHOOL...
I HAD SUCH A PRETTY FACE-- AND NOW, IT'S LIKE THIS.
NOBODY CAN EVER TELL WHAT I'M THINKING.
EVEN IF SOMEONE WANTED TO GET CLOSE...
SINKING INTO HER CONSCIOUSNESS, I CAN SEE...
THE THINGS SHE'S SEEN.
HA HA!
YEAH, I KNOW!
WHAT'S GOING ON WITH THE HOLE IN HER FACE?
DON'T YOU THINK IT'S...

AHH!
AHH!
WHOA!
TUUUUG!

HAAAH...
HUH?!
WAH!
ZLRP
AH, IT'S INSIDE...?!
HYUU
MY TENTACLE... IT'S GOING IN... SO DEEP...!
OKUTOU-SAN...
BA-DUMP
BA-DUMP
I WANT YOU TO FEEL INSIDE OF ME.
WOOOO
OOO
OOO
NG!
WHAT IS THIS...?
SHAKE
SHAKE
INSIDE OKUBO-SAN... FEELS AMAZING...!
IT'S SO VAST...!
SQUEAK
SQUEAK
ANNA.
I CAN'T BELIEVE THIS...
WILL YOU CALL ME "ANNA"?
BWOOOP...
くぽあ...

I CAN FEEL YOUR EYES ON ME.
?!
YOU WANT TO KNOW MORE ABOUT ME, DON'T YOU?
I'M SO HAPPY...
SQUEEZE...
YOU'RE ALWAYS WATCHING ME, RIGHT?
COME ON...
WHOA!
O-O-O-OKUBO-SAN?!
FLOP

HUH?!
UH... O-OKUBO-SAN?
UHM, HOW ARE YOU FEELING? WITH THE ANEMIA AND ALL THAT?
WE WERE ALL SO SCARED WHEN YOU COLLAPSED!
YOU DIDN'T SEEM PALE OR ANYTHING...

THAT'S...
ぽ
お..
HOLLOW...
BECAUSE I DON'T HAVE A FACE, RIGHT?

UHH...
N-NO, THAT'S NOT WHAT I MEANT!
HUH? IS SHE CRYING?
WAIT, SHE'S LAUGHING?!
OKU-TOU-SAN?
UHH...
AH, SORRY. I WAS STARING AGAIN...
THAT'S NOT IT.

YOU BROUGHT IT... BECAUSE YOU'RE HELPING OUT?
I SEE.
WELL THEN, THANKS.
WHAT'S WITH THAT REACTION?
IT'S NOT LIKE WE'RE ALL THAT CLOSE. IS SHE MAD...?
......
FWOOO

EEP!
OKUTOU-SAN?
IT'S KINDA EMBARRASSING HAVING YOU STARE INTO ME LIKE THAT...
COULD YOU PLEASE BACK OFF?
BOI-YOING
AH, DID I WAKE YOU?! I'M SORRY...!
......
NO...
JITTER JITTER
Okubo
UHM, I BROUGHT YOUR UNIFORM, OKUBO-SAN!
SEE, I'M HELPING THE NURSE OUT TODAY, SO...

31
Chapter

LIKE A MYSTERI-OUS ABYSS...
IT MAKES ME FEEL LIKE I COULD BE SUCKED IN...

Nurse's Office
WE HAVE TO GO RUN SOME ERRANDS...
CAN YOU LOOK AFTER THINGS, OKU-TOUSAN?
SURE!
Come to me with your health questions!
Nurse's Newsletter: May
SHLLP
SHLLP
SHLLP
SHLLP
SHLLP
SHLIDE
SHLIDE
SLIDE...
OKUBO-SAN...?
ARE YOU ASLEEP?
HARD TO TELL FROM HERE...
THIS EMPTY SPACE... ERM, I GUESS IT'S BETTER TO SAY HOLE?
WHERE DOES IT LEAD?
IT'S SO DARK, I CAN'T SEE THE BOTTOM.

Student Health Record
Jul. 201X
Class 2-B
Okutou Hasumi
Octopus Girl
• Four cephalopod-like tentacles sprout from her hips, while another four sprout from her lower back--making eight in total.
• The suckers on her tentacles have the ability to stick to things. As the suckers are clumps of muscles, their grip is strong, making it possible for her to stick to the ceiling.
• The tentacles are capable of delicate movement, though they do get tangled together now and then.
• When she gets nervous, the shape of her pupils change and slime seeps from her tentacles.
NYU!

NURSE
HITOMI'S
Monster
Infirmary
6

UNLIKE THE OTHERS, YOU ACTUALLY GET IT, DON'T YOU?
WHISPER...
HITOMI-SENSEI...
......
?

SO, WHAT IS IT ABOUT YOU THAT TICKS ME OFF SO MUCH?!
GLAARE
?
WHAT'S WRONG, TOBITA? YOUR STOMACH HURTING?

TATARA-SENSEI, LET'S HAVE A SWIMMING RACE!
I FEEL LIKE WITH MY BODY THIS HAIRLESS, I SHOULD BE ABLE TO WIN IN THE FREESTYLE FOR ONCE!
HA HA HA!
HUH?
EVEN SHAVED YOU'RE STILL ANNOYING.
THEY'RE SUCH GOOD FRIENDS!
Faculty Office

HA HA HA!
I SEE!
WELL, THAT'S A RELIEF!!

HEH!
IT IS!

NO MATTER HOW MUCH YOUR LOOKS CHANGE...
YOU'LL ALWAYS BE THE SAME MOJI-SENSEI.

HITOMI-SENSEI!
MATSU-SHIRO'S BODY IS FREEZING! WE NEED A TOWEL!
MOJI-SENSEI...
PLEASE CALM DOWN.

SNIFF...
SEN-SEI...
THERE'S NO NEED TO WORRY.
MATSU-SHIRO-SAN'S BODY TEMPERA-TURE IS NATURALLY LOW.

HUH?
I'M NOT HAIR... I MEAN, HURT...
PAT...

WHEEEW!

KER-SPLASH
YOU OKAY, MATSU-SHIRO?!
YOU DIDN'T SWALLOW ANY WATER, DID YOU?! DID YOU HIT YOUR HEAD?!

SPLOOSH

HEY, WHERE ARE YOU GOING?
WOBBLE WOBBLE WOBBLE
NO FLUF-FY...
NO LIFE...
WATCH IT--!!
MATSU-SHIRO?!
AH!
SHE FELL IN!
SPLOOSH
?!

THERE ARE MORE IMPORTANT THINGS THAN LOOKS, ANYWAY.
WAAAH...
GO FOR IT, TOBITA-SAN!
THEY DO SAY LOVE IS BLIND.
WELL, YOU ARE KIND OF BIASED.
YOU'RE SO INNOCENT!
NYAH!
MRR...
MRR...

SADNESS...
MY FLUFFY MOJI-SENSEI IS DEAD AND BURIED...
HE'S NOT DEAD! HE'S RIGHT HERE!
DESPAIIIR!
PUFF
PUFF
PUFF
PUFF
PUFF

THIS CHICK...
THE ONLY PART OF MOJI-SENSEI SHE LIKES IS HIS HAIR.
C'MON!
IT'S JUST FOR SWIM CLASS!
HIS FUR WILL GROW BACK IN THE FALL!

MOJI-SENSEI IS SURPRISINGLY YOUNG.
SQUEE!
WITH A NICE BODY... ♥
EEE!
I LIKED HIM BETTER BEFORE.
KYAA!
REALLY? ARE YOU KIDDING ME?
SQUEE!
HE'S ACTUALLY KINDA CUTE...
MURR...

OH, SO THEY'RE SUDDENLY BIG FANS?
YOU NEVER EVEN LOOKED AT HIM BEFORE!
BLUB
BLUB
BLUB
BLUB

HE'S STILL THE SAME OL' STUPID HAIRBALL!
JOLT
?!
HMM-PH!
WHISPER
WHISPER

DID YOU SPRAY WATER REPELLENT ON YOUR WINGS?
YEAH, YEAH-- WINGS GET HEAVY WHEN THEY TAKE ON WATER.
A GIRL FROM CLASS B EVEN HELPED ME GET THE BACKS.

OH, GOOD!
WELL ...

?!
I'LL BE YOUR SUBSTI-TUTE FOR SWIMMING CLASS!
WHO'S THAT ?!
WHO'RE YOU?!
I'VE SHAVED ALL MY HAIR.
THAT'S PRETTY SLICK.
WHAT THE HECK IS THIS?
HIS SKIN'S SO SHINY!
SURE, I WAS A LITTLE FREAKED OUT AT FIRST, TOO...

SOME MEN LOOK YOUNGER AFTER A SHAVE. IT'S NO BIG DEAL!
HA HA HA!
EVEN HIS LAUGH IS DIFFERENT!
BA-DUMP
BA-DUMP
MOJI-SENSEI... WHEN HE SHAVES, HE'S LIKE A DIFFERENT PERSON.
FIDGET
FIDGET

WHEN I THINK ABOUT IT...
IN A PRIVATE ROOM WITH A MAN
AND NOW HERE I AM GETTING ALL EMBAR-RASSED!!
WHA-HUH?!
TOBITA.
SO SOFT...

YAMMER YAMMER
HUH?
NO WAY!
WHO THE HECK ARE YOU?!
THERE'S NO WAY HE LOOKS LIKE THAT JUST 'CAUSE HE GOT A SHAVE, RIGHT?!
......
HIS CHARACTER DESIGN HAS CHANGED COM-PLETELY!!
OKAY, GUYS, SIMMER DOWN.
DA-DAAN
完全に不一致
COMPLETE MIS-MATCH

—THE FOLLOWING WEEK—

BIG PAPA BEAAAAR!
IT'S LIKE BEING WITH MY DAD!
AH HA HA!
YOUR DAD?!
I DO GET TOLD THAT I SMELL LIKE AN OLD MAN!
I'M ONLY ONE YEAR OLDER THAN YOU, THOUGH!
BA HA HA HA!
Nurse's Office
HEE HEE HEE!
IT'S JUST... YOU'RE SO BIG AND FLUFFY LIKE MY FATHER!
I'LL TAKE IT AS A COMPLIMENT, THEN!

AH, JEEZ!
I DIDN'T MEAN TO GO ON A RANT LIKE THAT!
AH HA HA...
NAH, IT'S FINE.
HEE-HEE!
MOJI-SENSEI...
BEING WITH YOU...
MAKES ME FEEL SO AT EASE.

BUT THERE ARE PLENTY OF ADULTS WHO ARE PERFECTLY COMFORTABLE LYING RIGHT TO YOUR FACE.
MY MOTHER'S SURGERY FEES?
OF COURSE THAT WAS A LIE! ★
PREFECTURAL POLICE
......
AND THERE ARE EVEN THOSE WHO WOULD PREY ON POOR, UNHAPPY SINGLE WOMEN LOOKING FOR TRUE LOVE!
OH WOW, THAT SOUNDS AWFUL...
TEARS OF BLOOD
SCRRRAPE
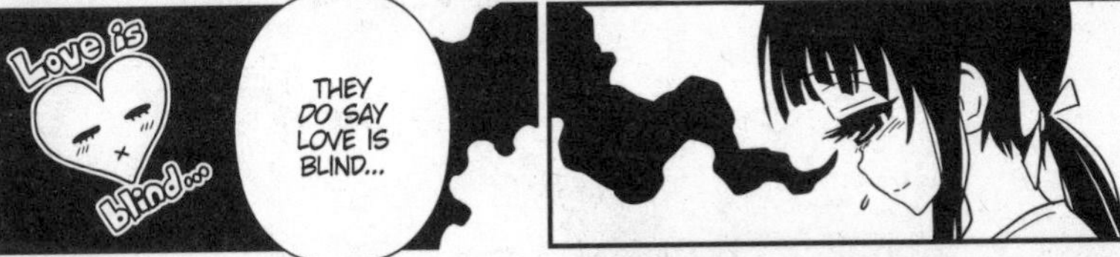
THEY DO SAY LOVE IS BLIND...
Love is blind...

DESPAIR...
I GUESS I JUST CAN'T SEE STRAIGHT WHEN IT'S MY OWN HEART AT STAKE!
IT'S A TOUGH SUBJECT FOR ME RIGHT NOW, ACTUALLY.
I SEE...
HUUH...♥
I HOPE YOUR BROKEN HEART HEALS QUICKLY.

I'M SORRY, BUT I JUST CAN'T PROMISE...
THAT I WON'T DO SOMETHING STUPID LIKE THAT AGAIN.
BUT I WILL TRY AND TAKE BETTER CARE OF MYSELF!
MOJI-SENSEI, YOU'RE SO CONSCIEN-TIOUS!
SO SINCERE.
VRO...
BA HA HA!
THERE'S NO POINT LYING.
NO ONE ALIVE COULD TRICK THAT ALL-SEEING EYE OF YOURS, HITOMI-SENSEI!
VRO
VRO
VRO..
THAT'S NOT TRUE.
I MEAN-- SURE, THERE AREN'T MANY KIDS WHO SUCCESSFULLY FAKE AN ILLNESS TO GET OUT OF CLASS...
MY TUMMY HURTS...
ER... ACTUALLY, I'M FINE.

HONESTLY, EVEN NOW...
I STILL RELIVE THAT MOMENT.

WHAT IF I HADN'T CAUGHT HER?

I DON'T KNOW IF I'LL EVER STOP THINKING ABOUT IT.

EVEN THOUGH IT'S JUST GYM CLASS, PEOPLE CAN STILL GET HURT.
KIDS TEND TO ACT BEFORE THEY THINK THINGS THROUGH.

OF COURSE.
I'M GLAD YOU COULD PROTECT ONE OF OUR STUDENTS.
BUT EVEN SO...
I WAS REALLY WORRIED...
WHEN IT HAPPENED.
PLEASE DON'T BE SO RECKLESS.
......

MOJI-SENSEI...
THAT BUMP ON YOUR HEAD DOESN'T HURT ANYMORE, DOES IT?
NAH, IT'S TOTALLY FI--
OH, WELL...
A BIT.
JUST SOMETIMES... LIKE ON RAINY DAYS IT HURTS-- BUT NOT EXCRUCIATINGLY SO.
THANKS FOR YOUR CONCERN, THOUGH.

YOU SEEM TO ENJOY IT, HITOMI-SENSEI.
UFU FU FU~!
I SO WANTED TO TRY THIS!
TRI~M
I CAN'T REACH MY BACK ON MY OWN, SO THIS IS A HUGE HELP.
HA! HA HA HA
THIS IS FUN!
YOUR BACK IS SOOOO BIG, IT'S EASY TO SEE THE PROGRESS I'M MAKING!
IT'S A BIT BRISTLY, BUT THE BLADE IS STILL CUTTING THROUGH.

HAVING TO TEACH SWIM CLASS ALL OF A SUDDEN MUST BE TOUGH.
AH, WELL, THE TEACHER WHO WAS SUPPOSED TO HEAD UP THAT CLASS GOT INJURED, SO IT CAN'T BE HELPED.
......

HUFF!♥
HUFF!♥
OOO!
AHAA-AAH...!♥
YOUR FUR IS FLYING OFF!
RRRRM RRRMM RAAAAAR

BA-DUMP
BA-DUMP
YES...
BA-DUMP
BA-DUMP
BA-DUMP

SQUEAK
MOJI-SENSEI...
IT'S SO... SO MUCH...

......
IT'S SO MUCH THICKER AND HARDER THAN I THOUGHT IT WOULD BE...

WELL...
I'M WILLING TO GIVE IT A TRY... IF YOU ARE...
SLIDE...
AHH! IT...
FEELS...
SO GOOD...
OHHHO...

HEE HEE!
YOU SAY THAT, BUT YOUR GRUMPY FACE...
TELLS ANOTHER STORY.
HUUH?!
CHIIRP
CHIIRP
CHIIRP
I'M NOT GRUMPY! THIS IS JUST MY DEFAULT EXPRESSION!

MOJI-SENSEI...
ARE YOU...
REALLY... OKAY WITH ME DOING THIS?
THIS SORT OF THING CAN BE EMBARRASSING FOR A GUY.
A LOT OF THEM AREN'T WILLING TO LET THEMSELVES BE SO... *VULNERABLE.*

MY... TYPE...?
IF I HAD TO PICK, I'D SAY... SOMEONE WHO'S CONSCIENTIOUS AND KIND... I GUESS?
THAT'S THE KIND OF LAME ANSWERS SHE GIVES ME WHEN I ASK ABOUT HER LOVE LIFE.
BUT I THINK SHE'S ACTUALLY TELLING THE TRUTH!

LEAN
IN ALL HONESTY...
IF YOU SAY YOU'LL ONLY SETTLE FOR NICE GUYS, YOU'RE GONNA END UP HURT.
THROWING HIS HANDS IN THE AIR.
AH, WELL...
SHE COULD DO WORSE THAN END UP WITH THAT HAIRBALL.
PFF!

I DON'T CARE AT ALL!!
TOBITA-SAN'S RUNNING AROUND LIKE A CHICKEN WITH ITS HEAD CUT OFF.
RRRIIIIIPP
WHAA...?! I-I-I AM NOT!!
RIPP
I J-J-JUST MESSED UP ON THIS WORK SHEET, SO I FIGURED I MIGHT AS WELL TEAR IT UP.
CHEEP! CHEEP!
I CAME ALL THE WAY TO THE FACULTY OFFICE TO FLUFF MOJI-SENSEI...
Faculty Office
BUT HE ISN'T HERE.

Character
Health
Love of Learning
Creation
July Activities Schedule
IT'S TOUGH TO ADMIT...
BUT THEY DO MAKE A GOOD PAIR, DON'T THEY?
ARE YOU STILL GOING ON ABOUT THAT?

......

WHAT WAS THAT ABOUT?
AND WHY AM I HIDING?

MOJI-KUN AND HITOMI-CHAN ARE CLOSE IN A... DIFFERENT WAY...
SLIDE...
......

WELL, THE PHYSICAL EDUCATION DEPARTMENT DOES DO A LOT OF HEALTH RE-LATED STUFF, SO IT MAKES SENSE.
SPIN SPIN
SPIN SPIN

SO THAT'S IT...
BUT...

THE WAY THEY WERE JUST NOW... IT SEEMED LIKE A LITTLE BIT MORE THAN THAT.
AREN'T YOU CURIOUS WHAT THEY WERE WHISPERING ABOUT?
SHURURU

FLU FFY
MOJI-SENSEI...
SLIIIDE
Faculty Office
MY PAPER...

ARE WE STILL ON FOR TONIGHT ...?
......
AH...

YES, OF COURSE!
TEE HEE!

WELL THEN-- SEE YOU IN MY OFFICE, AFTER ALL THE STUDENTS ARE ALL GONE...

—A WEEK EARLIER—

FLAAAAFF
SHADDUP! WHO YOU CALLING FLAT?!
HUH ?!
WAH!
UH... I'M SORRY...!
WHATEVER... MORE IMPOR-TANTLY...

IS THAT CHICK OKAY?
HAAH... HAAH...
SHIVER

MATSU-SHIRO-SAN?!
YOU'RE CHILLED TO THE BONE!!
fwRoooo
IS THAT IT...?

BONG
But isn't wearing her lab coat over her bathing suit even *more* erotic, in a way?
What a profound truth!
SEVERAL SECONDS IS PLENTY! IF YOU WASH THEM TOO MUCH, OR FOR TOO LONG, YOU COULD IRRITATE THE EYE.
I'M KINDA DISAPPOINTED SHE DIDN'T WEAR A BIKINI, THOUGH.
WHISPER...
BOYS ARE SO GROSS!
SNICKER...
BLEH!
ALL BOYS ARE LIKE THAT.
THEY'RE NOT THAT IMPRESSIVE.
HMPH!
THEY'RE JUST LUMPS OF FAT!

THAT'S TRUE, TOBITA-SAN!
YOUR BODY IS SO LEAN AND LIGHT! BEING SUPER FLAT ACTUALLY HELPS YOU FLY BETTER!
LEAD IN...
"ALL BOYS"?
IF I HAD BOOBS LIKE THAT, THEY'D JUST DANGLE WHEN I WENT FLYING.